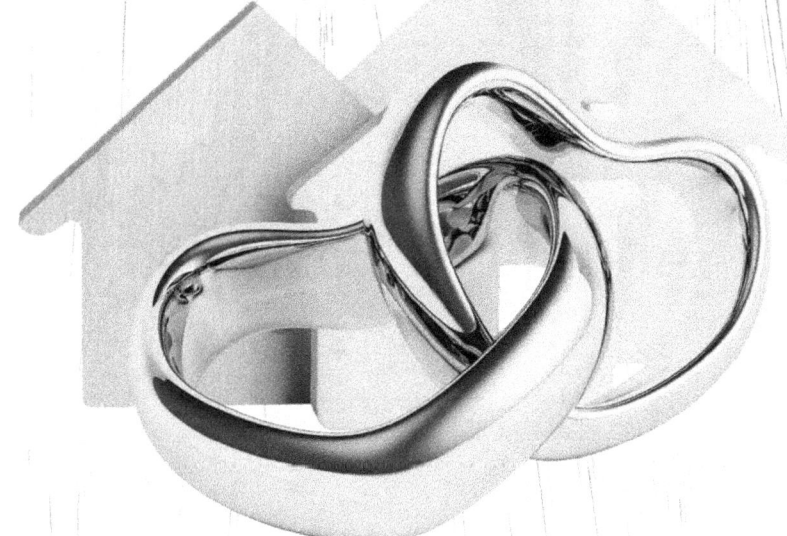

Divine Detours

When Hearts Find Their Way Home

#1 International Bestselling Author
Angela R. Edwards

Divine Detours

When Hearts Find Their Way Home

Angela R. Edwards

Pearly Gates Publishing LLC
INSPIRING CHRISTIAN AUTHORS TO BE AUTHORS

Pearly Gates Publishing, LLC, Harlem, GA (USA)

Divine Detours:
When Hearts Find Their Way Home

Scripture references are used with permission via Zondervan at Biblegateway.com.

ISBN 13: 978-1-948853-83-5
Library of Congress Control Number: 2024952969

For information and bulk ordering, contact:
Pearly Gates Publishing, LLC
Angela Edwards, CEO
P.O. Box 639
Harlem, GA 30814
pearlygatespublishing@gmail.com

Dedication

To all who believe in the
divine power of love:

May this story stoke the flame of faith
in your hearts, reminding you that true
love—like God's grace—is boundless.

Introduction: Where Faith and Love Intertwine

L ove frequently creates the most exquisite and complex patterns in the fabric of life, turning us in unexpected directions and taking us to places we never would have thought possible. *Divine Detours* is a testament to that truth. It's a story reminding us that sometimes, the most indirect routes can lead us to our true purpose and deepest connections.

Set against the backdrop of the city of Millbrook, Georgia, with its rolling hills, lush forests, and the historic Tabernacle Baptist Church, the tale begins with a chance encounter that would change two lives forever. It is here that we meet our protagonists, Chloe Thompson and Cyrus Thornton—two souls whose paths cross in a moment orchestrated by God.

With her caramel-colored eyes reflecting the depths of her faith and compassion, Chloe Thompson is a beacon of light in Millbrook. Raised in a modest home where love and service were valued above all else, Chloe has dedicated her life to sharing God's love, particularly through her work in the children's ministry at Tabernacle. Her open heart and unwavering faith have touched many lives, yet she guards her own heart, scarred by past relationships and wary of the vulnerability that true love demands.

Enter Cyrus Thornton, the prodigal son of Millbrook's most prominent family. With his chiseled features, seductively deep brown eyes, and confident bearing, Cyrus appears to be the epitome of worldly success. Yet beneath his polished exterior lies a soul searching for meaning, a heart yearning to reconnect with the faith of his youth. His return to Millbrook is more than a homecoming; it is a quest for redemption and purpose.

Their first meeting at a Fall Festival sets in motion a series of events that will challenge their beliefs, test their resolve, and ultimately reveal the transformative power of love rooted in divine grace. As their eyes meet for the first time during a haphazard moment, the words of 1 John 4:7-8 seem to echo in the air around them:

"Dear friends, let us love one another, for love comes from God. Everyone who loves has been born of God and knows God. Whoever does not love does not know God, because God is love."

That biblical truth becomes the cornerstone of their journey together, a reminder that love—pure, selfless, and grounded in faith—has the power to overcome even the most daunting obstacles. And obstacles, they soon discover, are plentiful on the path they've chosen to walk together.

From the outset, Chloe and Cyrus face opposition that threatens to tear them apart before their love can fully bloom. Cyrus' family, led by his formidable mother, Victoria Thornton, views Chloe as an unsuitable match for her son. She feels that Chloe's modest upbringing and commitment to ministry work are incompatible with the aspirational future she has in mind for her son. Victoria's faith is more a matter of social convention than heartfelt conviction, so she views Cyrus' choice of a mate as a threat to her carefully laid plans for her son's life.

That external pressure is compounded by internal struggles that both Chloe and Cyrus must confront. For Chloe, the intensity of her feelings for Cyrus is both thrilling and terrifying. She must learn to trust not only in him but also in God's plan for her life, opening her heart to love despite the risk of pain. Cyrus, caught between his growing love for Chloe and his sense of duty to his family, faces a choice that will define the man he will ultimately become. His journey back to faith, inspired largely by Chloe's unwavering devotion to God, becomes intertwined with his journey toward true love.

As their relationship deepens, Chloe and Cyrus discover that their love, anchored in shared faith, has the power to weather any storm. They cling to the promise found in 1 Corinthians 13, that *"love is patient and kind, not easily angered, and always perseveres."* In moments of doubt and trial, they turn to prayer, seeking guidance and reassurance in the face of mounting opposition.

Their story becomes a living testament to the power of faith-filled love to overcome even the most daunting obstacles. The journey is not without its setbacks: misunderstandings, moments of weakness, and the constant pressure of societal expectations threatening to drive them apart. Yet in those moments of trial, Chloe and Cyrus cling most fiercely to their faith and each other, embodying the truth that love can indeed conquer all when rooted in God.

Divine Detours is more than just a Christian love story; it is an exploration of the human spirit, a celebration of faith, and a reminder that love, in its purest form, is a reflection of The Divine. Their journey touches on themes that resonate with all of us: the struggle between duty and desire, the fear of vulnerability, the power of forgiveness, and the courage it takes to follow one's heart in the face of adversity. As we follow Chloe and Cyrus through the twists and turns in their relationship, we are reminded that sometimes, the path to true happiness and fulfillment is not a straight line but a series of divine detours, each one bringing us closer to our true purpose and to the love that God intends for us.

This book challenges us to look beyond the surface, to see the potential for growth and love in every encounter, and to trust in a plan greater than our own. It reminds us that love, when grounded in faith and nurtured with patience and understanding, has the power to bridge divides, heal wounds, and bring light to even the darkest of places.

As you embark on this journey with Chloe and Cyrus, prepare to be inspired, challenged, and ultimately uplifted. Their story will make you laugh, cry, and reflect on your own journey of faith and love. It will remind you that no matter how lost you may feel, no matter how many detours you may encounter, there is always a divine plan at work in your life.

Divine Detours is an invitation to open your heart to the possibilities of love, to strengthen your faith in the face of adversity, and to trust that even the most unexpected turns in life can lead to the most beautiful destinations. As you turn these pages, may you find hope in the darkest moments, strength in times of weakness, and, above all, a renewed belief in the transformative power of love—a love that comes from God and leads us back to Him because He is love.

Welcome to Millbrook. Welcome to the lives of Chloe and Cyrus. Welcome to a journey that will remind you that in love and faith, all things are possible. Let the 'Divine Detours' begin!

Table of Contents

Chapter One: A Spark of Hope

The gentle hum of conversation filled the air as Chloe stepped into the immense church hall. Her heart pounded with a mixture of anticipation and dread. The annual Fall Festival was in full swing, with cheerful decorations adorning every corner and the aroma of pumpkin spice wafting through the room. She smoothed down her pin-striped dress, took a deep breath, and plastered on a smile that she hoped didn't betray her inner turmoil.

Chloe's best friend and fellow choir member, Sarah, shouted across the room. "Chloe! You made it!" Sarah rushed over to give her a warm hug. Her enthusiasm was infectious, helping to melt away some of Chloe's tension.

"I wouldn't miss this for the world!" Chloe replied, trying to match Sarah's excitement. In truth, Chloe had contemplated staying home, curled up with *"I AM" Cares* by Bestselling Author Marlowe R. Scott and a cup of tea, but she knew that isolation wasn't the answer. It had been six months since Mark had walked out of her life, leaving her with a shattered heart and wavering faith. The church community had been her lifeline during those dark days, and she owed it to them—and to herself—to keep showing up.

Sarah looped her arm through Chloe's and guided her towards the refreshment table. "Come on. Let's get you some of Ms. Holden's famous apple cider. It'll warm you right on up!"

As they weaved through the crowd, Chloe couldn't help but notice the many couples in attendance. They held hands, laughed as they shared private jokes, and radiated genuine contentment. A familiar ache bloomed in her chest, prompting her to silently pray for strength to make it through the day.

'Lord, help me find joy in Your presence, even when my heart feels so empty.'

"Here you go, dear," Ms. Holden said as she handed Chloe a steaming cup of cider. Her kind eyes crinkled at the corners as she smiled. "It's good to see you here, Chloe. We've missed your beautiful voice in the choir."

Chloe felt a pang of guilt. "Thank you, Ms. Holden. I've missed singing, too. I promise I'll be back soon." As she turned away from the table, sipping the warm, spicy cider, she collided with a tall, solid form. The cup slipped from her grasp, but not before its contents splashed across a crisp white shirt. "Oh, no! I'm so sorry!" she exclaimed, mortified. She quickly grabbed a handful of napkins from the table and dabbed at the growing light brown stain. Her cheeks burned with embarrassment.

"Hey, no worries," replied a deep, gentle voice. "I'd say this shirt desperately needed some fall-themed tie-dye anyway, wouldn't you agree?"

When Chloe finally looked up, her eyes met a pair of kind brown eyes that crinkled at the corners with amusement. The man before her was tall, with curly black hair and a warm smile that made her heart skip a beat. She quickly pushed that feeling aside, reminding herself of the wall she'd so carefully constructed.

"I'm Cyrus," he said, extending his right hand. "And you are?"

"Chloe," she replied, shaking his hand briefly before stepping back. "I'm truly sorry about your shirt. Please, let me pay for the dry cleaning."

Cyrus waved off the offer with a chuckle. "Don't worry about it. Consider it my contribution to making this event more exciting. Besides, I now have an excuse to go home and change into something more comfortable. It seems I'm a bit overdressed for this occasion."

Chloe couldn't help but smile at his easy-going nature. It was refreshing but also terrifying. She knew all too well from the past how a man's charm could mask ulterior motives.

"So, Chloe," Cyrus continued, totally oblivious to her internal struggle, "are you a regular here at Tabernacle Baptist?"

She nodded in the affirmative, grateful for the quick shift in conversation. "Yes, I've been attending for about five years now. I'm usually in the choir, but I've been... taking a break lately."

Something in her tone must have given her away because Cyrus' expression softened. "Sometimes, we all need a little break to recharge our batteries. I'm sure your voice is missed, though."

Before she could respond, Pastor Merchant's voice boomed through the hall, calling everyone's attention. "Welcome, everyone, to our annual Fall Festival! Let's gather around and give thanks for this wonderful community and the blessings of the season."

As people started moving towards the center of the room, Chloe saw an opportunity to escape. "I should go find my friend," she said, already backing away from Cyrus. "Again, I'm sorry about your shirt."

"Wait!" Cyrus called out, causing her to pause. "Would you like to join me for the blessing? It would be nice to have a friendly face nearby."

She hesitated, torn between her instinct to retreat and the genuine warmth in Cyrus' eyes.

'Lord, give me wisdom,' she prayed silently.

After a moment, she replied, "Okay. Sure."

As they made their way through the crowd, she couldn't help but notice how Cyrus seemed to radiate a sense of peace. It was both comforting and unsettling, stirring feelings she had long since buried.

Pastor Merchant led the congregants in a heartfelt prayer, thanking God for the changing seasons and the constant love that sustains through life's ups and downs. His words struck a chord within Chloe, and tears formed in the corners of her eyes.

"Are you okay?" Cyrus whispered. His concern was evident.

She nodded, quickly wiping away a stray tear. "Yes, just... moved by the prayer."

As the crowd dispersed, Cyrus turned to face her fully. "Chloe, I hope this isn't too forward, but I'd love to get to know you better. Would you like to grab a coffee sometime this week?"

Her heart raced as fear and excitement warred within. "I... I... I don't know," she stammered. "I'm not really in a good place for... that sort of thing right now."

Cyrus' expression remained gentle and understanding. "I understand. How about this: Why don't we start as friends? No pressure. Just two people getting to know each other over a cup of coffee. And, if you're not comfortable, we can stick to chatting at church events. What do you say?"

She took a deep breath, taking his offer into consideration. Part of her wanted to run to protect herself from the possibility of more pain. The other part—a voice that sounded suspiciously like hope—

urged her to take a chance. "Okay," she finally said. "Friends. Coffee. I think I can manage that."

Cyrus' face lit up with a broad smile that seemed to brighten the entire room. "Wonderful! How about Wednesday afternoon at The Cozy Corner Café?"

Chloe nodded in agreement, feeling a flutter of something she hadn't experienced in months: anticipation. It was small... barely a whisper in the face of her fears—but it was there. They quickly exchanged telephone numbers, with Cyrus stating he would call on Monday to schedule their friend date before parting ways.

Later that night, as she knelt by the bed for her evening prayer, she poured out her heart to God.

"Lord, You know the pain I've carried. You know the doubts that have plagued me. I don't understand Your plan, but I trust You are with me. Please give me the strength to open my heart again and see the blessings You have placed in my life. And if Cyrus is meant to be a part of that, help me to be brave enough to find out. Amen."

As she climbed into bed, she felt a sense of peace wash over her. She didn't know what the future held, but for the first time in a long while, she was curious to find out. With a small smile, she closed her eyes—the memory of kind brown eyes and a cider-stained shirt following her into her dreams.

Chapter Two: A Taste of Hope

The soft glow of candlelight danced across the crisp white tablecloth as Chloe smoothed her royal blue dress for what felt like the hundredth time. L'Fleur, with its elegant décor and soft French music, was a far cry from the casual cafes and coffee shops where Cyrus and she had spent the past few weeks getting to know each other. Her heart fluttered with a mixture of excitement and apprehension as she glanced at the man sitting across from her.

Cyrus looked dashing in a tailored gray suit. His deep brown eyes were warm and inviting as he basked in Chloe's glow. "You look beautiful," he spoke softly. A gentle smile played on his lips.

Chloe felt a blush creep up on her cheeks. "Thank you," she replied, tucking her hair behind her ear. "You clean up pretty well yourself." As the waiter approached with menus, she sent up a silent prayer.

'Lord, give me the strength to be open to this experience. Help me to trust in Your plan.'

"Have you ever been to a French restaurant?" Cyrus asked as his eyes scanned the menu.

"No. This is a first for me. To be honest, I'm a little intimidated by all these fancy names," she admitted with a nervous laugh as she looked down at the menu.

"Well, how about we make it an adventure? We could close our eyes and point to something random on our menus!" he said with clear amusement.

His playful suggestion eased some of Chloe's tension. "That sounds like a recipe for disaster," she giggled. "Perhaps we would be better served if you recommended something. You seem to be experienced with this type of cuisine."

"I'd be honored," he replied with a playful French accent. "How about we start with the 'Soupe a l'Oignon Gratinee'? It's a delicious French onion soup. And then, for the main course, I'd recommend the 'Coq au Vin'—a classic chicken dish cooked in wine sauce."

As Cyrus ordered for both of them in impressively fluent French, Chloe found herself studying him. Over the past few weeks, she'd discovered he was a man who was kind, funny, and deeply committed to his faith. Still, a part of her held back, afraid to fully open her heart.

"A penny for your thoughts?" Cyrus asked, pulling her from her reverie.

She took a sip of water, which bought her a few seconds to gather her thoughts. "I was just thinking about how surreal this all feels," she admitted. "A few months ago, I couldn't imagine myself sitting in a place like this on a date..." Her voice trailed off.

Cyrus reached across the table, his hand hovering near hers but not quite touching—a gesture of support without pressure. "I know this is a big step for you, Chloe. I want you to know that I appreciate your courage in being here tonight."

His words touched something deep within her, and tears teased the corners of her eyes. "Oh, my. I'm so sorry," she said, blinking rapidly. "It's just..." She chose her next words carefully. "After Mark left, I thought that part of my life was over. I was so angry at him, at myself, and even at God. I couldn't understand why He would let me go through such pain."

Cyrus listened intently, with his eyes full of compassion. "Faith isn't about having all the answers," he said softly. "It's about trusting God has a plan, even when we can't see it. Your pain is valid, Chloe, and it's okay to question Him. But I believe God can use even our darkest moments to lead us to something beautiful."

Just then, their soup arrived. Steam rose in delicate swirls from the smooth, yellowy surface. Chloe felt a warmth that had nothing to do with the food.

"Thank you, Cyrus," she whispered. "Thank you for understanding and for not pushing me to be somewhere in life that I'm not ready to be yet."

As they savored the rich, creamy, comforting soup and crispy baguettes, their conversation flowed more easily as the evening progressed. Cyrus shared stories of his own struggles with relationships, faith, and times when he felt lost and alone. His openness and vulnerability touched Chloe, slowly chipping away at the walls she'd built around her heart. When their main courses arrived—the Coq au Vin for her and Boeuf Bourguignon for him—the rich aromas filled the air, reminding Chloe of the simple pleasures in life she'd been neglecting.

After taking her first bite, Chloe exclaimed, "This is amazing!" The tender chicken and flavorful sauce danced on her tongue.

Cyrus grinned. "I'm glad you like it. You know, there's something special about sharing a meal with someone special. It's intimate... it's nourishing—both for the body and the soul."

Those words resonated with Chloe, reminding her of breaking bread together as a family of faith at church. "It reminds me of communion," she mused. "You know... how something as simple as bread and wine can hold so much meaning."

Cyrus nodded as his eyes lit up. "Exactly! It's a beautiful metaphor for how God uses the ordinary to create the extraordinary."

As they continued to eat and talk, Chloe felt a sudden shift within. The fear and hesitation that had been her constant companions for so long began to recede, replaced by a tentative hope. She found herself laughing more freely, sharing more openly, and truly enjoying Cyrus' company.

When dessert arrived—a decadent chocolate soufflé to share—Cyrus raised his water glass in a toast. "To new beginnings," he said softly.

She clinked her glass against his. "To new beginnings," she echoed.

When they left the restaurant, the cool night air kissed Chloe's skin, causing her to shiver. Cyrus draped his jacket over her shoulders—a gentlemanly gesture that warmed her in more ways than one.

"Thank you for tonight, Cyrus," she said as they walked towards his car. "It was... more than I could have imagined."

He stopped suddenly and turned to face her. The streetlight cast a soft glow on his features as his eyes searched hers. "Chloe," he said tenderly, "I want you to know I care for you deeply. I understand that you're still healing, and I want to honor that. Just know I will take this as slowly as you need."

His words washed over her like a soothing balm. At that moment, she felt a surge of gratitude for many things, including Cyrus' patience, God's guiding hand, and the strength to take the next step. "Cyrus," she said, her voice barely above a whisper, "I care for you, too. Yes, I'm scared, but... I think I'm ready to see where this journey might lead us." Cyrus' smile lit up the night sky, adding millions more stars to the galaxy. Chloe sent up a silent prayer of gratitude.

'Lord, thank You for this moment, for this man, and for the hope You've rekindled in my heart. Guide us as we walk this path together.'

With a gentle, reassuring squeeze of her hand, Cyrus led her to his car. As they drove toward home, the city lights blurred past the window. Chloe felt a peace she hadn't known in months. The future was still uncertain, but for the first time in a long while, she was excited to see what it might hold.

That night, as she knelt by her bed to pray, her heart overflowed with thanks.

"Thank You, Lord, for Your endless love and grace. Thank You for Cyrus and for giving me the courage to open my heart again. Whatever comes next, I trust in Your plan."

As she drifted off to sleep, the memories of candlelight, shared laughter, and the promise of new beginnings followed her into her dreams.

Chapter Three: Family Ties and Trials

Chloe's heart raced as Cyrus' car pulled into the driveway of a stately two-story mansion. Manicured lawns and perfectly trimmed hedges framed the home, exuding an air of sophistication that made her feel instantly out of place. She smoothed down her floral dress, second-guessing her choice of attire for what felt like the hundredth time that morning.

"Ready?" Cyrus asked, his warm hand covering hers reassuringly.

She inhaled deeply and offered a silent prayer.

'Lord, give me strength and grace for this day.'

"As ready as I'll ever be!" she replied with a nervous smile.

As they approached the front door, it immediately swung open to reveal a statuesque woman with Cyrus' deep brown eyes and an expression that could freeze lemonade in an instant. "Cyrus, darling," she said, her voice as crisp as her pressed emerald green linen suit. Her gaze swept over Chloe, a flicker of disapproval in her eyes. "And you must be Chloe."

"It's nice to meet you, Mrs. Thornton," she stated, extending her hand. Mrs. Thornton took it briefly, her grip limp and dismissive.

"Please, come in," she instructed, turning on her heels without waiting for a response.

Cyrus squeezed Chloe's hand encouragingly as they followed his mother into a living room that looked like it belonged in a home décor magazine. Everything around was pristine, not a cushion out of place.

"Cyrus, your father is in his study. Why don't you go say hello?" Mrs. Thornton suggested. Her tone left no room for argument. "I'd like to have a little chat with Chloe."

As Cyrus reluctantly left the room, Chloe felt like a lamb being led to the slaughter. Mrs. Thornton's piercing gaze pinned Chloe to her seat.

"So, Chloe," she began, her voice dripping with false sweetness, "tell me about yourself. What is it that you do?"

"I work as a kindergarten teacher. I love working with children and—"

"A teacher?" she interrupted, her right eyebrow arching. "How... quaint. And your family? What do your parents do for a living?"

Chloe swallowed hard, feeling the sting of that woman's judgment. "My father is a carpenter, and my mother is a registered nurse."

Mrs. Thornton's lips pursed as if she'd tasted something sour. "I see. And how exactly did you meet my son?"

As Chloe recounted their meeting at the church event, she could feel Mrs. Thornton's disapproval growing with each word. She interrupted frequently, asking pointed questions about Chloe's background, education, and aspirations. With each answer, she felt smaller, less worthy of being in that grand house, and less deserving of Cyrus' affection.

"Well," Mrs. Thornton said, her tone dismissive, "I suppose Cyrus is going through a charitable phase. His desire to help the less fortunate is truly admirable."

Her words hit Chloe like a backhand slap. She blinked back tears, praying for composure.

'Lord, give me the strength to endure this with grace.'

Just then, Cyrus returned with his father—a distinguished-looking man with kind eyes. "Dad, this is Chloe," Cyrus said, his voice warm with affection.

Unlike Mrs. Thornton's, Mr. Thornton's' handshake was firm and welcoming. "It's wonderful to meet you, Chloe. Cyrus has told us so much about you."

As they moved to the dining room for lunch, Chloe couldn't help but notice the stark contrast between Cyrus' parents. While his father engaged her in genuine conversation, asking about her work and interests, Mrs. Thornton continued her subtle jabs and dismissive comments.

"Oh, Cyrus," she said at one point, "do you remember Caroline from the country club? She just returned from her studies abroad. She's such an accomplished young woman."

Chloe felt her heart sink, understanding the implication. Cyrus, however, seemed oblivious to his mother's machinations. "That's nice, Mom," he said absently. His eyes met Chloe's, followed by a warm smile.

As the afternoon wore on, Chloe found herself retreating inward. Her responses became shorter, and her smiles more forced. By the time they said their goodbyes, she felt emotionally drained.

Once settled in the car, Cyrus turned to look directly into her eyes. Concern was etched on his face. "Are you okay? You've been quiet."

She hesitated to respond, not wanting to come between Cyrus and his family. As she looked into his caring eyes, the dam broke wide open. "Your mother... she doesn't approve of me," she said, her voice barely above a whisper. "She made it clear that she doesn't think I'm good enough for you."

Cyrus' expression softened as he took her hand in his. "Chloe, listen to me. My mother..." He paused to find the right words before proceeding. "My mother has her own ideas about what my life should look like. But I'm a grown man, capable of making my own decisions about what—and who—I want in my life."

His words warmed her heart, but the doubt lingered. "But what if she's right? What if I'm not—"

"Stop right there," Cyrus interrupted gently. "You are kind, compassionate, and full of faith. Those are the qualities that matter to me. My feelings for you are growing stronger every day, and no one—not even my mother—can change that."

Long-held tears welled up in her eyes, a mix of relief and lingering hurt. "Thank you, Cyrus. I just... I want to be accepted by your family."

Cyrus pulled her into a comforting embrace. "Give it time, my sweet. My father already adores you, and my mother... well, she'll come around eventually. What matters most is how we feel about each other."

During the return trip home, she reflected on the day's events. It hadn't been the warm family welcome she'd hoped for, but Cyrus' unwavering support filled her with hope. She sent up a silent prayer of gratitude.

'Lord, thank You for bringing Cyrus into my life. Help me to trust in Your plan, even when the path seems difficult.'

That night, as she knelt by her bed, she prayed not only for herself but also for Mrs. Thornton.

"Lord, soften her heart. Help her to see beyond appearances and status. And give me the strength to respond with love, even in the face of rejection."

As she drifted off to sleep, she held onto Cyrus' words and the comfort of God's love. Whatever challenges lay ahead, she knew with faith and love, they could face them together.

Chapter Four: Blossoming Love

The gentle crash of waves against the shore provided a soothing backdrop as Cyrus and Chloe strolled hand in hand along the beach. The setting sun painted the sky in breathtaking hues of orange and pink, casting a warm glow on Cyrus' face as he turned to smile at Chloe. Her heart fluttered, still amazed at how far they'd come since that fateful day at the church festival.

"You know," Cyrus began, his voice soft and contemplative, "moments like these make me truly appreciate God's artistry. The way He paints the sky, the rhythm of the waves... it's all a testament to His love for us."

She squeezed his hand in response, feeling a surge of affection. "It's beautiful. And being here with you makes it even more special."

Cyrus stopped walking and turned to face her. His deep brown eyes reflected the golden light of the sunset. "Chloe," he said, reaching into his pocket, "I have something for you."

She found herself holding her breath as he pulled out a small velvet box. Opening it, he revealed a delicate silver rope necklace with a cross-shaped pendant and a small diamond in the center.

"I saw this and thought of you," he explained, his voice tender. "The cross represents our shared faith, which is the foundation of our relationship. And see how the diamond sparkles? That's to remind you of how brightly you shine in my life."

Tears welled up in her eyes as Cyrus fastened the necklace around her neck. "It's beautiful, Cyrus. Thank you," she whispered, touching the pendant gently.

As they continued their walk, the necklace proved to be a comforting weight against her skin. She marveled at how Cyrus always seemed to know exactly how to make her feel cherished. It wasn't just the gifts, though they were always thoughtful and sometimes lavish. It was the way he listened—truly listened—when she spoke and the way he remembered little details about her likes and dislikes. Plus, despite his busy schedule, he always made time for her.

A few days later, they found themselves at La Petite Maison—a charming French bistro that had become their favorite date spot. The intimate setting, with its soft candlelight and romantic music, created the perfect atmosphere for connection. As they savored their meals—Coq au Vin for Chloe, and Beef Bourguignon for Cyrus—their conversation flowed effortlessly. They touched on everything from their daily lives to their deepest hopes and dreams.

"You know," Chloe said, twirling her fork in the rich brown sauce, "I've been thinking a lot about my calling lately. I love teaching, but I feel like God might be nudging me towards something more."

Cyrus leaned forward. His interest was piqued. "What do you mean?"

She took a deep breath, sharing a thought she'd been nurturing for weeks. "I've been considering starting a faith-based after-school program for underprivileged children. Something that combines education with spiritual guidance."

Cyrus' face lit up with enthusiasm. "Chloe, that's an incredible idea! Your passion for teaching and strong faith makes you perfect for something like that!"

His immediate support warmed her heart. "You really think so? It's a big undertaking. I'm not sure I have what it takes."

Reaching across the table, Cyrus took her hand in his. "I believe in you, Chloe. And, more importantly, I believe that if this is God's plan for you, He will provide everything you need to make it happen."

Looking into his eyes, she felt a wave of gratitude wash over her. Not just for his support but for how their relationship deepened her faith and gave her the courage to dream bigger.

The following weekend, the couple curled up on Cyrus' couch with a bowl of popcorn between them as they settled in for a movie night. They chose a classic romantic comedy, but as the movie played, Chloe found herself more aware of Cyrus' presence than the plot.

Halfway through the movie, Cyrus paused it and turned to her. "Chloe," he said, his voice serious, "there's something I've been wanting to talk to you about."

Her heart rate quickened. "What is it?"

He took a deep breath and said, "These past few months with you have been the happiest of my life. You've brought so much joy... so much light into my world. And I've realized something..." He paused, and Chloe held her breath, hardly daring to hope for greater news.

"I love you, Chloe," Cyrus said softly, his eyes shining with emotion. "I love your kindness, your faith, and your passion for helping others. I love the way you challenge me to be a better man... a better Christian. I love everything about you."

As she processed each word, all her lingering doubts and insecurities melted away, replaced by a certainty she'd never felt before. "Oh, Cyrus," she whispered, her voice thick with emotion. "I love you, too. So much. You've shown me what it means to be truly cherished—to be loved not in spite of my flaws but because of who I am. You've helped me grow in my faith and in myself. I love you with all my heart." Cyrus pulled her into a tender embrace, and she sent up a silent prayer of thanks.

'Lord, thank You for bringing this amazing man into my life. Thank You for Your perfect timing and endless love.'

They spent the rest of the evening talking, laughing, and simply enjoying each other's presence. As the night grew late, they knelt together in prayer before Cyrus returned Chloe home, thanking God for

His blessings and asking for His continued guidance in their relationship.

In the days that followed, Chloe felt as though she was walking on air. Every moment with Cyrus seemed more precious and meaningful now that they'd expressed their love for one another. Their shared faith, which had always been the foundation of their relationship, seemed to deepen even further.

One evening, as they volunteered at the church's soup kitchen, Chloe watched Cyrus interact with the people they were serving. His kindness, his genuine interest in their stories, and the way he prayed with those who asked all reaffirmed why she'd fallen in love with him.

As they cleaned up afterward, Cyrus surprised her with another gift: a beautiful purple leather-bound journal. "I thought you could use this to plan your after-school program," he explained. "And to write down your prayer requests and reflections as you embark on this new journey."

She hugged him tightly, overwhelmed by his thoughtfulness. "Thank you, Cyrus, for the journal... and for believing in me."

"Always," he replied, kissing her forehead gently. "We're partners now, in both love and faith. Whatever challenges come our way, I promise we will face them together."

As she lay in bed that night—her new journal on the nightstand and the cross necklace around her neck—she reflected on how much her life had changed since that first meeting at the Fall Festival. What had started as a chance encounter had blossomed into a love story that was deeper and more fulfilling than she'd ever imagined possible.

She knew their journey together was just beginning and that there would be challenges ahead, but with their love for each other, their shared faith, and God's guidance, she felt ready to face whatever the future might hold.

After saying her nightly prayers, she drifted off to sleep. Her heart was full of gratitude and love , and she looked forward to whatever adventures tomorrow might bring with Cyrus by her side.

Chapter Five: A Weekend of Promise and Premonition

The gleaming façade of the 20-story Grand Horizon Hotel loomed before them as Cyrus' car pulled into the circular driveway. Chloe's heart fluttered with a mixture of excitement and apprehension. Their weekend getaway marked a significant milestone in their relationship, and she couldn't help but feel a twinge of nervousness.

"Are you ready?" Cyrus asked, his warm smile instantly calming her nerves.

She nodded, offering a silent prayer.

'Lord, guide us through this new chapter of our relationship.'

As they entered the opulent lobby, Chloe marveled at the massive crystal chandeliers and intricate marble floors. While Cyrus checked them in, she couldn't help but notice how he specifically requested adjoining rooms. His thoughtfulness in ensuring her comfort touched her deeply.

"I want you to feel completely at ease, Chloe," he said as they rode the elevator to the top floor. "This weekend is about us spending quality time together. Nothing more."

His words washed over her like a soothing balm, easing the last of her concerns. When they reached their rooms, Cyrus insisted on carrying her luggage inside and ensured she was settled in before retreating to his own room to freshen up.

That evening, they dined at the hotel's rooftop restaurant. The city's lights twinkled below them like earthbound stars. As they savored the exquisite meal, their conversation flowed effortlessly, touching on their hopes, dreams, and shared faith.

"Chloe," Cyrus said, reaching across the table to take her hand, "I want you to know how much I cherish you. Your faith, your kindness, your beautiful spirit... they mean the world to me."

Tears began to form in her eyes. "Oh, Cyrus, I feel the same way about you. You've shown me what true love and respect look like."

As the weekend progressed, the couple explored the city together, visited a nearby botanical garden, and even attended a local church service on Sunday morning. Throughout it all, Cyrus was the perfect gentleman: attentive, caring, and always mindful of Chloe's comfort.

The most memorable day of the trip was when they found themselves strolling hand in hand through the hotel's lush gardens. The air was heavy with the scents of roses and jasmine, creating an almost intoxicating atmosphere. As they paused by a bubbling fountain, Cyrus turned to face Chloe. His eyes were filled with an intensity that made her catch her breath.

"Chloe," he began, his voice soft but earnest, "these past few months with you have been the happiest of my life. I've never felt so connected to someone... so in tune with another person's heart and soul."

Her heart raced as she gazed up at him. "I feel the same way, Cyrus."

He pulled her closer, his arms encircling her waist. "I want you to know that I'm committed to you. To us. Whatever the future holds, I promise to always honor and cherish you."

As their lips met in a tender kiss, Chloe felt a surge of emotion wash over her. It was a moment of pure connection, their hearts beating as one. Yet, even as she reveled in the warmth of Cyrus' embrace, a tiny seed of unease took root in the back of her mind.

That evening, they decided to have a quiet night in. Cyrus ordered room service to her room, and they sat on the balcony, eating and watching the sunset paint the sky in vibrant hues. As they talked and laughed, Chloe marveled at how comfortable, safe, and cherished she felt with him.

"Chloe," Cyrus said softly, his eyes meeting hers, "I hope you know how much I respect you and your boundaries. I never want you to feel pressured or uncomfortable in any way."

His words touched her deeply. "Thank you, Cyrus. Your respect means everything to me. I've never felt so secure with someone before."

As the night wore on, their conversation turned to more serious topics: their hopes for the future, fears, and insecurities. In a moment of vulnerability, Chloe shared her past struggles with self-doubt and her journey to strengthen her faith.

"Wow! I'm so proud of you, Chloe," he said, squeezing her hand. "Your faith and your strength inspire me daily."

As they gazed into each other's eyes, Chloe felt that magnetic pull again, drawing them closer. Their lips met in a kiss that was both tender and passionate, filled with love and promise. It was a moment of deep emotional intimacy as their souls connected on a level she had never experienced.

When they finally parted, Cyrus rested his forehead against hers. "I love you, Chloe," he whispered. "And I promise to always be here for you, to support you and lift you up."

"I love you, too, Cyrus," she replied, her voice thick with emotion.

As she lay in bed that night, she reflected on how much her life had changed since meeting Cyrus. He had shown her a depth of love and respect she'd never known and always put her comfort and well-being first.

Yet, as she drifted off to sleep, that small seed of unease began to grow. Despite the beauty of their weekend together and the strength of their connection, she couldn't shake the feeling that challenges lay ahead that would test the very foundation of their relationship.

In her dreams that night, she found herself walking through a misty forest. Cyrus was ahead of her, his hand outstretched, beckoning her forward. But as she tried to reach him, the mist thickened, obscuring him from view. She called out, but her voice was swallowed by the denseness of the fog. When she finally broke through, she stood alone in a clearing, the echo of Cyrus' voice fading into the distance.

She woke with a start, her heart pounding. The dream left her with a lingering sense of foreboding—a vague but persistent feeling that something was about to change.

As they enjoyed their last morning together at the hotel, Chloe tried to shake off the unsettling feelings from her dream. They shared a leisurely breakfast, laughing and planning future dates. But even as she smiled and nodded, a part of her remained on edge, waiting for the other proverbial shoe to drop.

On the drive home, Cyrus sensed her sudden unease. "Is everything okay, Chloe?" he asked, his brow furrowed with concern.

She hesitated, not wanting to dampen the joy of their weekend. "I'm just... I don't know. I can't shake this feeling that something's going to happen. Something that might test us."

Cyrus reached over and took her hand, his touch reassuring. "Remember: I promised that whatever comes our way, we'll face it together. I believe our love and faith will see us through."

She smiled, drawing strength from his words and the warmth of his hand in hers. Yet, as they drove back toward their everyday lives, she couldn't help but wonder what those challenges are that lay ahead. Would their love be strong enough to weather the storms to come?

'Lord, please guide us through whatever trials we may face. Help us to stay rooted in Your love and truth.'

As the city skyline came into view, Chloe held onto the memory of their beautiful weekend together, hoping it would be a beacon of light in whatever darkness was to come.

Their love story was far from over, and she knew that with faith, trust, and the strength of their bond, they could overcome anything life might throw their way.

Chapter Six: A Test of Faith and Love

Cyrus stood in his mother's opulent living room, his hands clasped behind his back, gazing out of the floor-to-ceiling tinted windows. The manicured gardens beyond seemed a world away from the tension that filled the room.

"Cyrus, darling." His mother's voice cut through his thoughts. "I really think you should reconsider your association with that... Chloe girl."

He turned to face her, his jaw clenching slightly. "Mother, we've been over this. Chloe is not just some 'association.' We're committed to one another, and I love her."

Mrs. Thornton waved her hand dismissively. "Love is a strong word, dear. You hardly know the girl. Now, Rebecca Whitmore, on the other hand—"

"Rebecca?" Cyrus interrupted, his brow furrowing. "What does she have to do with this?"

His mother's eyes lit up, a smile playing at her lips. "Oh, you remember Rebecca, don't you? From the church fundraiser last month? Such a lovely girl, and she comes from an excellent family line. She's expressed quite an interest in you, you know."

Cyrus sighed, running his hand over his wavy hair. "Mother, I appreciate your concern, but I'm not interested in Rebecca or anyone else. I'm with Chloe."

"But darling," Mrs. Thornton persisted, her voice taking on a pleading tone, "you haven't even given Rebecca a chance. She's accomplished, well-connected, and shares our values. Surely you can see how much more suitable she would be for you than **her**?" She emphasized 'her,' continuing to show her disdain for her son's choice of a mate.

Cyrus felt an instant flicker of irritation. "More suitable? Mother, Chloe is kind, compassionate, and has a faith deeper than anyone I've ever met. How is that not suitable to you?"

Mrs. Thornton stood and crossed the room to place a hand on her son's arm. "Cyrus, I only want what's best for you. You have such a bright future ahead of you. Don't you think you owe it to yourself to explore all your options before settling for just anyone?" He opened his mouth to protest, but his mother continued, her voice softening. "All I'm asking is that you meet with Rebecca. Just once. For me. Is that really too much to ask?"

Cyrus hesitated, torn between his loyalty to his mother and his love for Chloe. The thought of meeting another woman felt like a betrayal, but the pleading look in his mother's eyes tugged at his heart. "Fine," he said finally, his voice tight. "One meeting. But that's all, Mother. I won't lead Rebecca on, and this doesn't change anything between Chloe and me."

Mrs. Thornton beamed, patting his cheek. "Oh, that's divine! That's all I ask, darling. You'll see. Everything will work out for the best."

A heavy weight settled in his chest as Cyrus left his mother's house. He knew he should tell Chloe about the meeting with Rebecca, but the thought of hurting her or causing her to doubt their relationship made him hesitate.

'Lord,' he prayed silently, *'guide me. Help me navigate this situation without compromising my integrity or hurting the one I love.'*

Over the next few days, the impending meeting with Rebecca weighed heavily on Cyrus' mind. He found himself growing distant and distracted, his thoughts a constant whirlwind of both guilt and confusion.

Chloe noticed the change almost immediately. As they sat in their favorite coffee shop, she reached across the table to take his hand. "Cyrus, is everything okay? You seem... I don't know... far away somehow after the last visit with your mother."

Cyrus forced a smile, squeezing her hand. "I'm fine, just a bit stressed with work. Nothing to worry about." The lie tasted bitter on his tongue, but he couldn't bring himself to tell her the truth. Not yet. Not until he figured out how to handle the situation. Chloe nodded, but he could see the concern lingering in her eyes... almost like she knew. He hated himself for putting that worry there. He despised being the cause of her anxiety.

As the days passed, Cyrus' internal struggle intensified. He threw himself into his work, using it as an excuse to create some distance between himself and Chloe. He told himself it was temporary, just until after the meeting with Rebecca. Then he would explain everything, and they would move past this bump in the road. Yet, with each canceled date and shortened phone call, he could feel Chloe's confusion and hurt growing. Her texts became more hesitant, and her voice became more uncertain when they spoke.

"Cyrus," she said one evening, her voice small over the phone, "have I done something wrong? You've been so distant lately, and I can't help but feel like you're pulling away from me."

His heart nearly stopped at the pain in her voice. "No, Chloe, of course not. You haven't done anything wrong. I'm just... I'm dealing with some things right now. I promise: It's not you."

"Can you talk to me about it?" she asked, a note of hope in her voice. "Whatever it is, we can face it together, remember?"

Cyrus closed his eyes, fighting back tears and the urge to confess everything right then and there. "I... I can't right now. But soon. I promise. I just need a little time to sort things out."

The silence that followed was heavy with unspoken words and growing doubt.

"Okay," Chloe said finally, her voice barely above a whisper. "I'm here when you're ready to talk."

Cyrus felt a deep ache in his chest as he ended the call. He knew he was hurting Chloe. He knew that his silence and distance were causing her pain. But the thought of telling her the truth about Rebecca—of admitting to his moment of weakness in agreeing to his mother's request—filled him with shame.

"*Lord,*" he prayed, sinking to his knees beside his bed, "*I've made a mess of things. I know I should be honest with Chloe, but I'm afraid of losing her. Please, give me the strength to do what's right.*"

The day of the meeting with Rebecca finally arrived, and Cyrus felt sick to his stomach—literally. After a brief stint in the bathroom, he managed to dress mechanically, his movements slow and deliberate as he tried to delay the inevitable.

As he drove to his office, his mind raced. He thought of Chloe and the love and trust in her eyes when she looked at him. He thought of his mother, her expectations, and the pressure she placed on him. And he thought of Rebecca—an innocent party in the mess he'd created.

Once in the parking lot, Cyrus sat in his car for a long moment, his hands gripping the steering wheel. He closed his eyes and took a deep breath. "This ends today," he said aloud in the confines of the car. "No more lies. No more hiding. I love Chloe, and it's past time I stood up for our relationship."

With newfound resolve, he stepped out of his car. He would meet with Rebecca, explain the situation, and apologize for any misunderstanding. Then he would go to Chloe, confess everything, and pray that she could forgive him.

They agreed to meet at a local restaurant a few doors from the office. With each step he made, Cyrus felt a weight lifting from his shoulders. He knew the road ahead wouldn't be easy, but he was ready to face whatever came next with honesty and faith.

'Lord,' he prayed silently as he walked briskly toward the restaurant, 'give me the courage to speak the truth and the wisdom to make things right.'

With that, Cyrus caught sight of Rebecca, greeted her with a smile, pushed open the restaurant door, and followed her inside. He was as ready as he could be to face the consequences of his actions and fight for the love he knew was worth everything.

Chapter Seven: Shattered Trust

The gentle patter of raindrops against Chloe's bedroom window mirrored the tears that had been threatening to fall all week. She curled up tighter in her oversized armchair, clutching a mug of lukewarm tea that she'd barely touched. The warmth and joy she'd felt during her and Cyrus' weekend getaway seemed like a distant memory now, replaced by a gnawing ache in her chest that she couldn't shake.

"Why, Cyrus?" she whispered to the empty room, her voice cracking. "What changed?"

It had been a week since they'd returned from the Grand Horizon Hotel—a week of increasingly brief phone calls, canceled plans, and vague excuses. The man who had held her close under the stars as he promised eternal love and devotion now felt like a stranger.

She closed her eyes, fondly remembering the tender moments they'd shared. Cyrus' gentle touch, his reassuring words, and the way he'd looked at her were the most precious things in the world. "I'll never hurt you, Chloe," he'd said, his deep brown eyes sincere and full of love. "You can trust me with your heart." A bitter laugh escaped her lips. How quickly those promises had crumbled.

She set down her mug and reached for her Bible, seeking comfort in the familiar verses. Her fingers traced the well-worn pages, landing on Proverbs 3:5-6:

"Trust in the Lord with all your heart and lean not on your own understanding; in all your ways submit to Him, and He will make your paths straight."

"I'm trying, Lord," she whispered, tears finally spilling over. "But it hurts so much. Help me understand. Light that which is in the darkness."

As she prayed, memories of the past week flooded her mind. The way Cyrus had pulled away when she'd tried to hug him after church on Sunday. The distant look in his eyes when they'd met for coffee, as if his mind were a million miles away. The growing silence during their phone conversations, punctuated by his distracted "Mm-hmms" and "Yeah, sures."

With each passing day, she'd felt the wall around her heart growing higher... stronger. It was a defense mechanism she knew all too well: protect yourself before you get hurt. But even as she built those walls, a part of her railed against them. This was Cyrus, after all—the man who had shown her what true love and respect looked like... the man who had promised to never cause her pain.

"Maybe I'm overreacting," she said aloud, trying to convince herself. "Maybe he's just stressed with work, like he said."

Yet and still, the knot in her stomach tightened, refusing to be ignored. There was something more going on. There was something Cyrus wasn't telling her. The thought of him keeping secrets from her, especially after all they'd shared, felt like a betrayal in itself.

She stood, suddenly restless, and began pacing her small apartment. Her eyes landed on the silver cross necklace Cyrus had given her, lying on her dresser. She picked it up, running her fingers over the delicate pendant. It had been a symbol of their shared faith, of the depth of their connection. Now, it felt heavy in her hand... a reminder of promises that seemed to be slipping away.

"Lord," she prayed aloud, clutching the necklace to her chest, "if this relationship isn't meant to be, give me the strength to let go. And if it is, please help Cyrus open up to me. Help us find our way back to each other."

As the days passed, Chloe threw herself into her work at the kindergarten, grateful for the distraction.

The children's laughter and innocence were a balm to her troubled soul, reminding her of the simple joys in life. But in the quiet moments, when the children were napping or otherwise engaged in activities, the doubts crept back in.

Had she imagined the depth of Cyrus' feelings?

Had she been so desperate for love that she'd seen what she wanted to see, rather than the truth?

Those thoughts made her feel naïve and foolish.

By Friday—nearly two weeks after their return from the hotel—she'd reached her breaking point. Cyrus had canceled their dinner plans yet again, citing a last-minute work commitment. The excuse rang hollow, adding to the mountain of doubt and hurt that had been building.

"I can't do this anymore," she told her reflection in the bathroom mirror, her eyes red-rimmed from crying. "I need answers."

With a determined set to her jaw, she made a decision: she would go to Cyrus' office and surprise him. Maybe if she could just see him and talk face-to-face without the barrier of a phone, they could sort things out. Maybe, just maybe, they could find their way back to the love and trust they'd shared.

She freshened up, adding a couple of squirts of White Diamonds perfume to her neck after changing into a pretty sundress—the one Cyrus had once said rested beautifully against her petite frame—and headed downtown. The early evening air was warm and fragrant with blooming flowers, a stark contrast to the turmoil in her heart.

As she approached Cyrus' office building, she saw him exit through the revolving doors. Her heart leaped at the sight of him, handsome in his crisp black suit. She raised her hand to wave, a smile starting to form on her lips, but the smile froze and then crumbled as she noticed his attention was focused squarely on a woman waiting near a restaurant door. She was tall and elegant, with perfectly long braided hair. Chloe recognized her immediately: Rebecca Whitmore, a regular at their church. Cyrus greeted her with a warm smile—one that used to be reserved solely for Chloe.

Time seemed to slow as she watched them engage one another in front of a restaurant. Their body language was relaxed... familiar. This was no chance encounter, no impromptu business meeting. This was a **date**!

Chloe stood rooted to the spot where she'd stopped, unable to move, unable to breathe. The world around her faded away, leaving only the image of Cyrus and Rebecca entering the restaurant, his hand resting lightly on the small of her back as he guided her through the door.

In that moment, all her fears and doubts crystallized into a single, devastating truth: Cyrus had lied to her. He had canceled their plans and pushed her away, all for this. For **her**.

The tears came then, hot and relentless. She turned and ran, not caring where she was going, just needing to get far away. Away from the sight of Cyrus with another woman. Away from the shattered remains of her trust and love.

She found herself in a small park, collapsing onto a bench as sobs wracked her body. The cross necklace felt like it was burning against her skin. She yanked it off, holding it in her trembling hand.

"Why, God?" she cried out, not caring who might hear. "Why did You let me believe in this love if it wasn't real? How can I trust anyone again?"

As the sun set, casting long shadows across the park, Chloe sat there, feeling more alone than she ever had before. The woman who had met a man who gave her such hope and determination was gone, replaced by someone who felt broken, betrayed, and lost.

In the gathering darkness, she closed her eyes and whispered a prayer, her voice barely audible. "Lord, I don't understand Your plan right now. I'm hurt and angry and so... so confused. But I know You're with me, even in this pain. Please, give me the strength to face whatever comes next. Help me find my way back to Your light."

With a deep, shuddering breath, Chloe stood. The path ahead was uncertain, shrouded in the pain of betrayal. But as she took her first tentative steps towards home, she clung to the hope that somehow, someway, God would see her through the darkness. She hoped and prayed that one day, she would find the strength to trust and love again.

Chapter Eight: Shattered Promises

The coffee shop bustled with its usual afternoon crowd, the aroma of freshly brewed espresso filling the air. But for Chloe, sitting at a corner table, the familiar scents and sounds were a stark contrast to the turmoil raging within her. Her hands trembled slightly as she clutched her mug, her eyes fixed on the door.

When Cyrus walked in, his familiar smile faltered as he caught sight of Chloe's expression. He approached the table, confusion evident in his eyes. "Chloe? What's wrong?" he asked, sliding into the seat across from her.

Chloe inhaled deeply, steeling herself for the conversation ahead. "I saw you, Cyrus," she said sternly. "Last Friday, when you told me you had to work late. I saw you with Rebecca at that fancy restaurant downtown."

The color drained from Cyrus' face, his mouth opening and closing as he struggled to find words. "Chloe, I... it's not what you think. Let me explain what—"

"Explain what, Cyrus?" Chloe interrupted, her voice gaining strength and volume. "Explain how you lied to me? How you've been pushing me away for weeks, only to spend time with another woman?" Tears welled up in her eyes as the full weight of her emotions crashed over her. "I trusted you, Cyrus. I believed in us. I thought... I thought you were different."

Memories flooded her mind—their first meeting at the church festival, the tender moments they'd shared, the promises whispered under starlit skies.

Each recollection now tainted with the bitter sting of treachery.

"Do you remember what you told me that night at the hotel?" Chloe asked, her voice cracking. "Let me remind you. You said you'd never hurt me. You promised to always be honest with me. Was that all a lie, too?"

Cyrus reached across the table, attempting to take her hand, but she pulled away. "Chloe, please. It wasn't a date. My mother—"

"Your mother?" Chloe scoffed, the pieces suddenly falling into place. "Of course. She never approved of me, did she? So, what? She set you up with Rebecca? And you just went along with it?"

"It wasn't at all like that," Cyrus pleaded. "I was trying to appease her. I thought if I met with Rebecca once, my mother would back off. I never meant for it to hurt you."

Chloe shook her head, a cynical laugh escaping her lips. "But it did hurt me, Cyrus. Your lies, your distance... do you have any idea how that felt? To wonder what I'd done wrong? To question every moment we've shared?" She paused, taking a shaky breath. "I loved you, Cyrus. I gave you my heart and trust. I believed in the future we talked about, the life we were planning together. And you threw it all away for what? To make your mother happy?"

Cyrus' eyes filled with regret. "Chloe, I'm so sorry. I made a terrible mistake. But I love you. What I feel for you is real. Please, give me a chance to make this right."

For a moment, Chloe allowed herself to consider his words. The love she felt for Cyrus was still there, but a deep ache pained her now. As she looked into his eyes, she saw not just remorse but a fundamental weakness she hadn't noticed before.

"No," she said quietly, a sense of calm settling over her. "I won't be anyone's second choice, Cyrus. I won't compete with Rebecca or any other woman your mother deems more suitable. And I certainly won't be with someone who can't stand up for our relationship."

Cyrus' face crumpled. If it were a glass vase, it would have shattered into a million pieces. "Chloe, please. I'll talk to my mother. I'll make her understand. Just give me a chance to fix this... mess."

Chloe stood, gathering her purse and belongings. "I'm sorry, Cyrus, but I can't. Trust is everything to me, and once it's broken... I don't know if it can be repaired." She reached into her purse to grab the silver cross necklace he had given her. Gently, she placed it on the table between them. "I thought this was a symbol of our love, our shared faith. But now I realize it was just another empty promise."

Cyrus stared at the necklace, his eyes filling with tears threatening to fall. "Chloe, please. Don't do this. I love you with all my heart. We can work through this."

For a fleeting moment, Chloe's resolve wavered. The urge to reach out, to comfort him, to believe in his words one last time was almost overwhelming. But then she remembered the sight of him with Rebecca, the weeks of lies and distance, and the fault of his mother in it, and her heart hardened once more.

"Goodbye, Cyrus," she said softly. "I hope you find happiness, whether it's with Rebecca or someone else. But it won't be with me."

With those final words, Chloe turned and walked out of the coffee shop, leaving behind not just Cyrus, but also the dreams and hopes they had shared. As the door closed behind her, she felt a curious mixture of pain and liberation.

The busy street outside was a blur as Chloe walked, her mind reeling from the confrontation. Part of her wanted to run back, to give Cyrus another chance, to cling to the love they shared. But a stronger part—the part that valued her self-worth and dignity—propelled her forward.

She found herself in the small park where she had sought solace the night she saw Cyrus with Rebecca. Sinking onto a nearby bench, Chloe finally allowed the tears to fall freely. She cried for the love she had lost, for the future that would never be, and for the trust that had been shattered.

As the sun began to set, casting long shadows across the park, Chloe's tears finally subsided. She looked up at the sky, streaked with brilliant oranges and pinks, and felt a small spark of hope ignite in her heart.

"Lord," she whispered, her voice hoarse from crying, "I don't understand Your plan right now. This pain... it's almost unbearable. But I trust that You have a purpose for everything, even this heartbreak. Please, give me the strength to move forward, to heal, and to love again someday."

As she spoke those words, Chloe felt a sense of peace wash over her. The road ahead would be difficult and filled with moments of doubt and longing, but she knew, deep in her soul, that she had made the right decision. She deserved a love that was honest, unwavering, and strong enough to withstand any challenge... and parent.

Standing, Chloe took in a deep breath of the evening air. The weight of her confrontation with Cyrus still pressed heavily on her heart, but alongside it was a newfound sense of self-respect and determination.

"This isn't the end," she told herself firmly. "It's a new beginning."

With those words, Chloe began the long walk home. Each step took her further from the life she had imagined with Cyrus, but also closer to a future filled with possibilities.

As the stars began to twinkle in the darkening sky, Chloe held onto her faith, knowing that somewhere out there, a man worthy of her love and trust was waiting.

Chapter Nine: Healing Hearts and Second Chances

The crisp autumn air nipped at Chloe's cheeks as she strolled through the park, leaves crunching beneath her feet. Three months had passed since that fateful day in the coffee shop when she had walked away from Cyrus, leaving behind not just a man but a future she had once believed in with all her heart.

Those past months had been a whirlwind of emotions: grief, anger, confusion, and slowly, tentatively, hope. Chloe had thrown herself into her work at the kindergarten, finding solace in the innocent laughter of children. She had rekindled old friendships and made new ones, filling her evenings with book clubs and volunteer work at the local women's shelter.

And yes, she had started dating again.

Tonight was date number five since the breakup. As Chloe approached the restaurant, she took a deep breath and smoothed down her peach-colored dress.

'Lord,' she prayed silently, *'guide me through this evening. Help me to be open to new possibilities.'*

Mitch, her date for the evening, was already waiting at the table. He stood as she approached, greeting her with a warm smile. "Chloe, you look lovely," he said, pulling out her chair.

As they settled into conversation over appetizers, Chloe found herself comparing Mitch to Cyrus. Where Cyrus had been passionate and intense from the start, Mitch was steady and calm. Where Cyrus' faith had burned bright, Mitch's seemed more of a quiet, personal matter.

'Stop it,' Chloe chided herself. *'It's not fair to compare every man to Cyrus.'*

Yet, even as she engaged in pleasant conversation with Mitch, discussing their shared love of classic literature and community service, Chloe's mind kept drifting. She remembered lazy Sunday afternoons spent with Cyrus, debating technology and dreaming of the future. She recalled the way his eyes would light up when he talked about his work and the passion in his voice when he prayed.

As the evening drew to a close, Chloe knew with a sinking heart that there wouldn't be a second date with Mitch. He was kind, intelligent, and by all accounts a good man, but the spark wasn't there. The connection she longed for remained elusive.

Walking home alone, Chloe's steps slowed as she passed the coffee shop where she and Cyrus had shared so many moments. Through the window, she could see couples laughing and friends chatting. Their lives were moving forward while she felt stuck in place.

Suddenly, a familiar figure caught her eye. Cyrus was there, sitting at their old table, a book open in front of him. For a moment, Chloe's breath caught in her throat. He looked up, seemingly as if he knew she was there. Their eyes met through the glass.

Time seemed to stand still. Chloe saw the recognition in Cyrus' eyes as he started to rise from his seat. But before he could make a move, she turned and hurried away, her heart pounding, threatening to fly out of her chest and stain her peach-colored dress crimson red.

That night, as Chloe knelt by her bed to pray, tears flowed freely. "Lord," she whispered, "I thought I was moving on. I thought I was healing. But seeing him... it still hurts so much. Please, help me find peace that surpasses all understanding. Help me to truly let go."

As the weeks turned into months, Chloe continued to date. Each encounter left her feeling hollower than the last. She went through the motions, smiling and nodding at appropriate times, but her heart remained closed off, protected behind walls built of past hurts and lingering love.

One crisp Sunday morning, nearly a year after the breakup, fate intervened once again. Chloe walked into church, her mind preoccupied with lesson plans for the coming week. She didn't notice him at first, as she was too focused on finding a seat. But then, she heard his voice, deep and familiar, greeting someone nearby. Chloe froze, her eyes scanning the room until they landed on Cyrus. He was standing near the front, engaged in conversation with Pastor Merchant.

As if once again sensing her gaze, Cyrus turned her way. Their eyes met across the crowded room, and Chloe felt her heart skip a beat. He looked good—older somehow, more mature. There was a seriousness in his eyes that hadn't been there before.

Throughout the service, Chloe found it hard to concentrate. Her mind kept drifting to Cyrus, wondering what he was thinking and if he was as affected by her presence as she was by his.

As the congregation began to file out after the final hymn, Chloe steeled herself for an awkward encounter, but Cyrus made no move to approach her. She felt a mixture of relief and disappointment.

It wasn't until the church had nearly emptied that Cyrus finally made his way over to her. "Chloe," he said softly, his voice sending a shiver down her spine. "It's good to see you."

Chloe nodded, not trusting herself to speak. Up close, she could see the emotions playing across Cyrus' face: regret, hope, and something deeper that made her heart race.

"I've missed you," Cyrus continued, his words rushing out as if he couldn't hold them back any longer. "Every day since you walked away, I've thought about you. About us. I know I hurt you, and I can never apologize enough for that. But Chloe, I still love you. I never stopped loving you."

His words hung in the air between them, heavy with meaning and possibility. Chloe felt tears pricking at her eyes, a year's worth of suppressed emotions threatening to overflow.

"Cyrus," she began, "I... I don't know what to say. This past year has been... difficult. I've tried to move on, to open my heart to others. But the truth is, no one has ever compared to you." Hope flared in Cyrus' eyes, but Chloe held up a hand, needing to finish. "But I'm not the same person I was a year ago. The pain of what happened... it changed me. I don't know if I can trust like that again."

Cyrus nodded, understanding in his eyes. "I know I have no right to ask for another chance," he said softly, "but Chloe, if you're willing, I'd like to try. To show you that I've changed, too. That I've learned from my mistakes and grown stronger in my faith and in myself."

As Chloe looked into his eyes, she felt the walls around her heart begin to crumble. The love she had tried so hard to bury was still there, as strong as ever. But alongside it was a new wisdom that she'd prayed for and a hard-earned understanding of her own worth and the kind of love she deserved.

"I can't make any promises," she said finally. "But... maybe we could start with coffee? As friends?"

The smile that lit up Cyrus' face was like the sun breaking through the clouds. "I'd like that," he said more excitedly than intended. "Very much."

As they walked out of the church together, Chloe sent up a silent prayer.

'Lord, I don't know where this path leads, but I trust in Your plan. Guide us. Protect our hearts. And help us to love with wisdom and grace.'

Yes, their future was uncertain, filled with both promise and potential heartache, but as Chloe looked at Cyrus, she felt a spark of hope ignite in her heart. Perhaps with time and faith, they could build something even stronger than before—a love tempered by adversity, rooted in trust, and guided by the unwavering light of God's grace.

Chapter Ten: Rekindled Flames

The soft glow of candlelight flickered across the table, casting warm shadows on Chloe's face as she sat across from Cyrus in an intimate corner of their favorite restaurant. It had been three months since that fateful Sunday at church when they'd agreed to try again, starting with coffee as friends. Those casual meetings had slowly evolved into longer conversations, shared laughter, and a cautious rekindling of the love they'd once shared.

Tonight felt different, charged with energy that made Chloe's heart race. Cyrus reached across the table, gently taking her hand in his. "Chloe," he began, his voice soft but filled with conviction, "I need you to know the whole truth about what happened with Rebecca."

Chloe tensed slightly. The memory of that painful time was still raw. She nodded, encouraging him to continue.

Cyrus took a deep breath. "My mother... she never approved of our relationship. She saw you as a distraction from the future she'd planned for me. When she learned about Rebecca's interest in me, she saw an opportunity." He paused, regret etched across his features. "She pressured me to meet with Rebecca, insisting it was just a friendly dinner. I foolishly agreed, thinking I could appease her without jeopardizing what we had. But in doing so, I betrayed your trust and our love." Tears fell from Chloe's eyes as he continued. "I should have stood up to my mother and made it clear that you were the only woman I wanted to be with. My weakness cost us a year of happiness, and I'll regret that for the rest of my life."

Chloe squeezed his hand, her voice barely above a whisper. "Thank you for being honest with me, Cyrus. It means more than you know."

A moment of silence passed between them, heavy with unspoken emotions. Then Chloe spoke again, her voice stronger. "I need to be honest with you, too. This past year... I tried to move on. I dated other men, thinking I could find what we had with someone else." Cyrus' hand tightened around hers, but he remained silent, listening intently. "But no matter how hard I tried, I could never connect with anyone the way I did with you. Every date felt hollow. Every conversation was superficial. My heart... it was always with you, Cyrus."

Tears flowed freely now—from both of them. Cyrus stood, moving around the table to kneel beside Chloe's chair. He took both her hands in his, looking up at her with eyes full of love and remorse.

"Chloe, I swear to you: You are the only woman I want to spend my life with. I've learned from my mistakes. I've grown stronger in my faith and in myself. If you'll have me, I promise to stand by you, to cherish you, and to love you with every fiber of my being for as long as I live."

Chloe's heart swelled with emotion. She cupped Cyrus' face in her hands, her thumbs gently wiping away his tears. "Oh, Cyrus," she whispered, "I love you, too. I never stopped loving you."

Their lips met in a tender and passionate kiss, a physical manifestation of the love and longing they'd carried for each other over the past year. When they finally parted, both were breathless, their faces flushed with emotion.

Cyrus stood, pulling Chloe to her feet and into a tight embrace. They stood there for a long time, swaying slightly, reveling in the feeling of being in each other's arms once again.

"Chloe," Cyrus murmured into her hair, "there's something else I need to say." He pulled back slightly, reaching into his pocket. Chloe's breath caught as he sank down on one knee, presenting a small red velvet box. "Chloe Renee Thompson," Cyrus began, his voice filled with love, "you are the most beautiful, kind, and loving woman I have ever known. Your faith inspires me, your strength amazes me, and your love completes me. I know we've been through trials, but they've only strengthened my love for you. I want to spend the rest of my life proving to you how much you mean to me." He opened the box, revealing a stunning diamond ring that sparkled in the candlelight. It was as if every candle in the dimly lit room aimed its flame directly at the ring. "Will you marry me?"

Chloe gasped, her hand flying to her mouth as tears of joy spilled down her cheeks. The ring was dazzling—a 3-karat diamond set in a delicate white gold band, its brilliance a testament to Cyrus' love and commitment to her.

"Yes, yes, yes! Yes, Cyrus, I'll marry you!"

The entire restaurant erupted into spontaneous applause. The couple hadn't realized they were the center of attention.

With hands that trembled slightly, Cyrus managed to slip the ring onto her finger. It fit perfectly, as if it had always been meant to be there. He then stood, gathering Chloe into his arms and spinning her around, both of them laughing and crying with joy.

As Cyrus set her down, Chloe looked up at him, her eyes shining with love and hope for their future. "I love you, Cyrus," she said softly. "With all my heart."

"And I love you, my beautiful Chloe," Cyrus replied, resting his forehead against hers. "Forever and always."

They shared another kiss, this one filled with promise and the excitement of their journey ahead.

As they left the restaurant hand in hand, Chloe sent up a silent prayer of gratitude.

'Thank You, Lord, for Your infinite wisdom and grace. Thank You for bringing Cyrus back into my life and for the love we share.'

The cool night air kissed their faces as they stepped outside. The stars twinkled overhead like a celestial blessing on their engagement. Chloe's ring caught the light of a nearby streetlamp, sending prisms of color dancing across their joined hands.

"What are you thinking?" Cyrus asked softly, noticing the contemplative look on Chloe's face.

She smiled up at him, her heart full to bursting. "I'm thinking about how far we've come and how excited I am for our future together. I'm thinking about the family we'll build, the ministry we'll share, and the life we'll create side by side."

Cyrus pulled her close, pressing a kiss to her forehead. "We have so much to look forward to, my love. And I promise you once again: Whatever challenges we face, we will face them together. With God's grace and our love, we can overcome anything."

As they walked towards his car, plans and dreams tumbling from their lips, Chloe felt a sense of peace and rightness settle over her. The pain of the past year faded away, replaced by the joy and hope of the present and the promise of a beautiful future.

Their once-fractured love story had been rewritten by God's grace and their unwavering faith in each other. As Chloe looked at the man beside her—her fiancé, her partner, her soulmate—she knew their greatest adventure was just beginning.

With hearts full of love and spirits buoyed by faith, Chloe and Cyrus stepped forward into their future, hand in hand, ready to face whatever life may bring... together.

Chapter Eleven: Confronting the Past

Chloe's heart raced as she stood on the doorstep of the Thornton family's imposing mansion. The weight of the diamond ring on her finger gave her strength—a tangible reminder of the love and commitment she shared with Cyrus. Taking a deep breath, she rang the doorbell, steeling herself for the confrontation ahead.

Mrs. Thornton answered the door, her perfectly coiffed appearance starkly contrasting the surprise that flickered across her face. "Chloe," she said, her voice cool and controlled. "What an unexpected pleasure. Cyrus isn't here at the moment."

"I know," Chloe replied, her voice mirroring Mrs. Thornton's. "I'm here to speak with you, Mrs. Thornton. May I come in?"

Reluctantly, Mrs. Thornton stepped aside, allowing Chloe to enter the opulent foyer. The air was thick with tension as they made their way to the sitting room, the click of Mrs. Thornton's heels echoing off the marble floors. As they settled into plush armchairs, Chloe took a moment to gather her thoughts. The conversation she'd had with Cyrus the night before played in her mind, his confession about his mother's manipulations fueling her determination.

"Mrs. Thornton," Chloe began, her voice calm but firm, "I think it's time we had an honest conversation about your attempts to undermine my relationship with Cyrus."

Mrs. Thornton's eyebrows rose, a feigned innocence crossing her face. "I'm sure I don't know what you mean, dear. I've only ever wanted what's best for my son."

Chloe leaned forward, her gaze unwavering. "With all due respect, Mrs. Thornton, we both know that's not entirely true. Cyrus has told me everything—about how you pressured him to meet with Rebecca and constantly tried to push us apart."

A flicker of anger flashed in Mrs. Thornton's eyes. "Now, see here, young lady. You have no right to come into my home and make such accusations. Cyrus is my son, and I know what's best for him. You're simply not suitable for someone of his standing."

Those words stung, but Chloe refused to be intimidated. She thought of the love she and Cyrus shared, of the faith that had brought them back together. Drawing strength from that, she pressed on.

"Mrs. Thornton, I understand that you want the best for Cyrus, but have you considered that maybe, just maybe, God has a different plan? That He brought Cyrus and me together for a reason?"

Mrs. Thornton scoffed. "Don't bring God into this. This is about Cyrus' future and his potential. You're holding him back from greatness!"

Chloe shook her head. A sad smile formed on her lips. "That's where you're wrong. Our relationship isn't just about us. It's about our shared faith and desire to serve God together. We've kept Him at the center of everything we do." She paused, her voice softening. "Mrs. Thornton, I love your son. Not for his status or his potential but for who he is. I love him for his kind heart, unwavering faith, and his passion for helping others. And he loves me, not despite my background, but because of who I am and the values we share."

Despite her best efforts, Mrs. Thornton's composure began to crack, her carefully maintained façade slipping. "You don't understand. I've worked so hard to give Cyrus every advantage. I won't let you get in the way of that."

"But at what cost?" Chloe challenged. "Your son's happiness? His ability to make his own choices? Mrs. Thornton, Cyrus is a grown man, capable of deciding his own future. And he's chosen me, just as I've chosen him."

The older woman's eyes flashed with anger. "You ungrateful girl! After everything I've done for my son, you dare to come here and lecture me? I could destroy you with a single phone call, ruining any chance you have at a future in this town!"

Chloe felt a surge of righteous anger but held it in check. "Is that really the kind of person you want to be, Mrs. Thornton—someone who uses threats and manipulation to get their way? Is that the example you want to set for Cyrus?"

Mrs. Thornton fell silent, her face a mix of emotions: anger, frustration, and something that almost resembled fear.

Chloe continued, her voice gentle but firm. "I'm not here to fight with you or to drive a wedge between you and Cyrus. I'm here because I love your son and desire nothing more in this situation than to find a way for you and me to move forward. But that can only happen if you're willing to let go of your preconceptions, get to know me for who I am, and truly see Cyrus and me for who we are." She held up her left hand, the engagement ring catching the sunlight that beamed through the window. "Cyrus asked me to be his wife, and I've said yes. We're going to build a life together, Mrs. Thornton. I hope that you'll be a part of that life, but that's a choice only you can make."

Mrs. Thornton's eyes widened at the sight of the enormous ring, a mix of emotions playing across her face. For a long moment, silence hung heavy in the air between them.

Finally, Mrs. Thornton spoke, each word barely audible. "He... really... loves... you... doesn't... he?"

Chloe nodded, her eyes filling with tears. "Yes, he does. And I love him more than I ever thought possible."

Mrs. Thornton seemed to deflate. The fight within had finally ended. "I... I need time to process this. Please, I think it's best if you go now."

Chloe stood, smoothing down her dress. "I understand. Thank you for listening, Mrs. Thornton. I pray that in time, you'll see that Cyrus and I are truly meant to be together." She paused as she walked towards the door, turning back to face the older woman. "And Mrs. Thornton? I forgive you. For everything. Because that's what my faith teaches me to do."

With those final words, Chloe walked out of the Thornton mansion, her head held high. As she stepped into the warm sunshine, she felt as if a heavy weight had finally been lifted from her shoulders. For the first time since meeting Cyrus' mother, Chloe felt truly free. She took a deep breath, savoring the sense of victory and liberation that washed over her. That confrontation had tested her strength, faith, and love for Cyrus. And she had passed with flying colors!

As she walked down the driveway, her phone buzzed with a text from Cyrus: "So, how did it go? Are you okay?"

A smile spread across her face as she typed her reply: "It went better than I expected! I'll tell you everything soon. I love you."

With each step, Chloe felt stronger and more confident in her love for Cyrus and their shared future. She had faced her greatest fear and emerged victorious. Whatever challenges lay ahead, she knew she and Cyrus could overcome anything with God's grace and their unwavering love.

As she reached her car, Chloe paused momentarily to look back at the Thornton mansion. A prayer of gratitude and hope rose in her heart.

'Thank You, Lord, for giving me the strength to stand firm in my faith and my love. Please soften Mrs. Thornton's heart and help her to see Your plan for us.'

With a deep sense of peace, Chloe drove away, leaving behind the shadows of the past and moving forward into the bright promise of her future with Cyrus. Their love story, once threatened by doubt and manipulation, now stood stronger than ever—a testament to the power of faith, forgiveness, and unwavering commitment.

Chapter Twelve: A Union of Hearts

The warm spring breeze carried the scent of blooming flowers as Chloe and Cyrus strolled hand in hand through the gardens surrounding Tabernacle Baptist Church. Their eyes sparkled with excitement as they envisioned their upcoming wedding day.

"I can't believe we're really doing this," Chloe said, her voice filled with childlike wonder. "It feels like a dream."

Cyrus squeezed her hand, his smile radiant. "The best kind of dream, my love. One that's coming true."

As they walked, they discussed the myriad details of their wedding plans. The venue was an easy choice, as Tabernacle Baptist held a special place in both their hearts. They laughed as they debated flower choices, finally settling on a mix of white roses and lavender, symbolizing their pure love and devotion.

A shadow crossed Chloe's face as they sat down to finalize the guest list. "Cyrus," she began hesitantly, "what about your mother? Do you... do you want to invite her?"

Cyrus' expression grew serious. "I've been thinking about that," he replied softly. "I know she's treated you poorly in the past, and I wouldn't blame you if you didn't want her there, but..."

"But she's your mother," Chloe finished for him.

He nodded. "More than that, I believe not inviting her would give the devil a foothold to disrupt our union every chance he got. We're starting our life together, and I want it to be built on forgiveness and love, not resentment."

Chloe was quiet for a moment, her heart conflicted. She thought of the confrontation with Mrs. Thornton, of the hurtful words and manipulative actions of the past. But she also thought of her faith and the teachings of forgiveness and grace. "You're right," she said finally, looking up at Cyrus with a small smile. "We should invite her. Even if she chooses not to come, we'll know we did the right thing."

Cyrus pulled her into a tight embrace, his voice thick with emotion. "Thank you, Chloe. Your forgiving heart never ceases to amaze me."

The next day, Cyrus stood in his mother's sitting room, his posture straight and determined. Mrs. Thornton sat primly on the edge of her chair, her face a mask of cool indifference.

"Mother," Cyrus began, his voice firm but respectful, "I'm here to personally invite you to my wedding. Chloe and I both want you to be there."

Mrs. Thornton's eyebrows arched. "Oh? And what makes you think I'd want to attend such an... ill-advised event?" She twisted her nose as if she'd smelled something horrendous.

Cyrus inhaled deeply and exhaled an audible sigh, steeling himself. "Because despite our differences, you're my mother. And because Chloe and I are building a life together—one based on love, faith, and mutual respect. We want you to be a part of that life—if you're willing."

He continued, outlining their plans for the future: their shared ministry goals and their dreams of starting a family. As he spoke, he saw something flicker in his mother's eyes—a mix of surprise and, perhaps, grudging respect.

When he finished speaking, his mother was quiet for a long moment. Finally, she replied, her voice softer than he'd heard in years. "I... I'll consider it, Cyrus. That's all I can promise for now."

It wasn't at all the enthusiastic acceptance he'd hoped for, but it was a start. He'd extended the proverbial olive branch. As he left, he sent up a silent prayer of thanks and hope.

The weeks that followed flew by in a flurry of preparations. Chloe and Cyrus threw themselves into the details, from selecting the perfect invitations to choosing the music for their first dance. Each decision brought them closer, their excitement growing with each passing day.

They spent evenings poring over seating charts, debating the merits of chocolate versus vanilla cake (they settled on a compromise: chocolate with vanilla frosting), and deciding whether to partake in the traditional wedding vows or write their own. Through it all, their love deepened, strengthened by the shared purpose of building a life together.

As the big day approached, Chloe often thought of Mrs. Thornton. The invitation had been sent, but no RSVP had been received. She tried not to let it dampen her joy, focusing instead on the love that surrounded them, the support of their friends and church family, and their own unwavering commitment to each other.

Finally, the wedding day arrived. Chloe stood at the back of the church, her heart pounding with anticipation. Her white gown flowed around her like a cloud, the delicate lace veil framing her radiant face. She thought of the journey that had brought her to this moment—the ups and downs, the challenges overcome, and the love that had blossomed and grown stronger with each trial.

As the music swelled and the doors opened, Chloe began her walk down the aisle, escorted by her tall and handsome father. Her eyes locked with Cyrus', seeing in them all the love and promise of their future together. The church was filled with the faces of loved ones, each smiling face a testament to the community that had supported their love.

As she neared the front, she couldn't help but notice the empty seat where Cyrus' mother should have been. A mix of emotions washed over her: disappointment, a twinge of hurt, and a strange sense of peace. They had reached out to her, but she didn't reach back. Mrs. Thornton had chosen resentment for Chloe over love for her only son.

When Chloe reached Cyrus at the altar, taking his hand in hers, she pushed thoughts of his mother aside. This moment was about them and the sacred vows they were about to make before God and their loved ones.

The pastor's voice rang out clear and strong in the sanctuary: "Dearly beloved, we are gathered here today in the sight of God to join together this man and this woman in holy matrimony..."

Chloe and Cyrus gazed deeply into each other's eyes, their hearts full of love and hope for the future. As they prepared to say their vows, Chloe prayed silently for their marriage, future, and, yes, even Cyrus' mother.

"I, Cyrus, take you, Chloe, to be my wedded wife," Cyrus began, his voice strong and sure. "To have and to hold, from this day forward, for better, for worse, for richer, for poorer, in sickness and in health, to love and to cherish, till death do us part, according to God's holy ordinance; and thereto, I pledge myself to you."

Chloe's voice trembled slightly as she repeated the vows, her heart overflowing with emotion. "I, Chloe, take you, Cyrus, to be my wedded husband..."

As they exchanged rings—the symbols of their eternal love and commitment—Chloe felt a sense of rightness settle over her. The absence of Cyrus' mother, while sad, couldn't diminish the joy of the moment. Their love, rooted in faith and strengthened by adversity, was a testament to God's grace and the power of forgiveness.

"By the power vested in me, I now pronounce you husband and wife," the pastor declared. "What God has joined together, let no one put asunder. You may kiss your bride."

As Cyrus leaned in to lift Chloe's veil and seal their union with a kiss, Chloe's heart soared. The church erupted in applause, the sound of joy and celebration washing over them. Hand in hand, they turned to face the congregation, ready to begin their new life together.

Walking down the aisle as husband and wife, Chloe and Cyrus were enveloped in the love and support of their community. The absence of one person couldn't overshadow the abundance of love that surrounded them.

As they stepped out into the sunlight, confetti raining down around them, Chloe knew that whatever challenges lay ahead, they would face them together. Their love story, once threatened by doubt and opposition, now stood as a beacon of hope and faith— a testament to the transformative power of love, forgiveness, and unwavering commitment to each other... and to God.

Epilogue: A Love That Endures

The bright afternoon sun filtered through the kitchen window, casting a golden glow on Chloe as she stood at the counter, preparing an after-school snack for her children. The sound of laughter drifted in from the backyard, where five-year-old Cullen chased his little sister Carmel around the swing set.

Chloe smiled to herself, her heart full of gratitude for the life she and Cyrus had built together. It hadn't always been easy, but their love, strengthened by faith and perseverance, had carried them through every challenge.

As if summoned by her thoughts, Cyrus appeared in the doorway, his tie loosened after a long day at the office. "How are my favorite people doing?" he asked, wrapping his arms around Chloe from behind and planting a kiss on her cheek.

"We're blessed, as always," she replied, leaning into his embrace. "How was your day, love?"

Cyrus sighed contentedly. "Productive. We closed that big deal I've been working on with the company in France. God's timing is perfect, as usual!"

Their conversation was interrupted by the pitter-patter of little feet as Cullen and Carmel burst into the kitchen, clamoring for their father's attention. Cyrus scooped up both of them, one in each arm, peppering their faces with kisses as they giggled uncontrollably.

As Chloe watched her family, she couldn't help but marvel at how far they'd come. The early years of their marriage had been filled with challenge after challenge that tested their faith and resolve. There had been financial struggles when Cyrus first started his business—months of living on a shoestring budget and fervent prayers for provision. Chloe remembered nights spent hunched over their worn Bible, seeking guidance and comfort in the Psalms.

But through it all, their love had only grown stronger. They had learned to lean on each other, find joy in simple things, and trust in God's plan even when the path seemed uncertain.

The arrival of Cullen had brought new challenges and immeasurable joy. Chloe's decision to become a stay-at-home mother had been met with raised eyebrows from some, but she and Cyrus knew it was the right choice for their family. When Carmel joined their family two years later, their happiness felt complete.

As Cyrus helped the children wash up for dinner, Chloe's mind drifted to the day they had decided to homeschool. It had been a daunting prospect at first, but now she couldn't imagine it any other way. The opportunity to shape their children's education and instill in them the values that were so important to their family was a privilege she cherished every day.

"Mommy, may I say the blessing tonight?" Cullen asked as they gathered around the dinner table.

"Of course, sweetheart," Chloe replied, smiling at her son's eagerness. They joined hands and bowed their heads as Cullen's small voice filled the room.

"Dear God, thank You for this food and for our family. Please help us to be kind and to love others like Jesus does. Amen."

"Amen," the family echoed, his parents' hearts warmed by the simple, sincere prayer.

As they ate, Cyrus and Chloe listened attentively to their children's chatter about their day: Cullen's excitement over the history lesson on ancient Egypt, and Carmel's pride in the watercolor painting she had created.

"You know," Cyrus said during a lull in the conversation, "I was thinking about how blessed we are. This house, my job, our health—they're all gifts from God."

Chloe nodded, understanding the weight of his words. "And we need to be good stewards of those gifts," she added. "To use them to honor God and to help others."

It was a conversation they had often, a reminder to themselves and their children that their blessings came with responsibility. They had established a tradition of regularly volunteering at the local homeless shelter and tithing faithfully to their church and various charities.

After dinner, as Cyrus helped with the dishes, Chloe reflected on how their relationship had evolved over the years. The conflicts of the past—his mother's initial disapproval and the doubts and insecurities they had both faced—seemed like distant memories now.

Mrs. Thornton eventually came around, won over by her son's undeniable happiness and her grandchildren's infectious joy. While the relationship with Chloe wasn't perfect, it had grown into one of mutual respect and even genuine affection.

As the evening wound down, the family gathered in the living room for their nightly devotional. It was a nightly tradition they had started when Cullen was just a toddler, a way to center their day on God's Word and to teach their children the importance of faith. Cyrus read a passage from Proverbs, his deep voice soothing as he explained the meaning in terms the children could understand. Chloe watched her family, her heart swelling with love and gratitude.

Later, after the children were tucked into bed with bedtime stories and prayers, Chloe and Cyrus sat on the porch swing, enjoying the peaceful evening.

"Do you ever think about how different our lives could have been?" Chloe asked, her head resting on Cyrus' shoulder.

Cyrus was quiet for a moment, his arm tightening around her. "Sometimes," he admitted. "But then I look at you, at our children, at everything we've built together, and I know this is exactly where we're meant to be."

Chloe smiled, intertwining her fingers with his. "I'm so proud of you, you know. The way you've built your business... how you've stayed true to your values, even when it wasn't easy."

"I couldn't have done it without you," he replied. "Your support and faith in me have been my strength through every challenge."

They sat in comfortable silence, watching as the first stars appeared in the darkening sky. Chloe thought about the journey that had brought them to that moment: the ups and downs, the lessons learned, and the love that had only grown deeper with each passing year.

"You know," Cyrus said softly, "sometimes I think about that day at the church festival when we first met. Did you ever imagine we'd end up here?"

Chloe laughed softly. "Honestly? No. But I'm so grateful that God had this plan for us, even when we couldn't see it."

As they headed inside, hand in hand, Chloe sent up a silent prayer of thanks for the love that had brought them together, for the faith that had sustained them, and for the family they had created.

Their story wasn't perfect. No real love story ever is. But it was theirs to live. The power of love, faith, and perseverance is as old as time. And, as they faced the future together, Chloe knew that whatever challenges lay ahead, their love—rooted in faith and strengthened by years of shared joys and trials—would see them through.

In the quiet of their home, surrounded by the evidence of their shared life and love, Chloe and Cyrus embraced, their hearts beating as one. Their journey was far from over, but they faced it with joy and anticipation, secure in their love for each other and their unwavering faith in God's plan.

And so, as another day drew to a close in the life they had built together, Chloe and Cyrus looked to the future with hope and gratitude, ready to embrace whatever blessings and challenges God had in store for them—together... always together.

As You Think About Love...

The following ten thought-provoking questions aim to deepen your understanding of how love, faith, and honesty intertwine in Chloe and Cyrus's journey, challenging them to reflect on the complexities of Christian relationships in the face of personal, familial, and societal obstacles.

Explore those themes through the lens of 1 John 4:7-8. The questions invite you to consider how divine love manifests in human relationships and how faith can guide individuals through life's challenges, ultimately fostering personal growth and a deeper connection with God.

1. How does Cyrus's journey of rediscovering his faith through his relationship with Chloe reflect the idea that "Everyone who loves has been born of God and knows God"?

_____

_____

_____

_____

_____

_____

_____

_____

_____

_____

_____

_____

_____

_____

2. In what ways does Chloe and Cyrus's love story challenge societal expectations, and how does this relate to the Christian concept of being "in the world but not of the world"?

_____

_____

_____

_____

_____

_____

_____

_____

_____

_____

_____

_____

3. How do the obstacles Chloe and Cyrus face, particularly from Cyrus's family, test their understanding of love as described in 1 Corinthians 13?

_____

_____

_____

_____

_____

_____

_____

_____

_____

_____

_____

_____

_____

4. In what ways does the story explore the tension between honoring one's parents and following God's calling, especially in Cyrus's case?

_____

_____

_____

_____

_____

_____

_____

_____

_____

_____

_____

_____

5. How does Chloe's past experience with heartbreak influence her approach to love and faith in her relationship with Cyrus?

_____

_____

_____

_____

_____

_____

_____

_____

_____

_____

_____

_____

6. How does the narrative demonstrate that love, as described in 1 John 4:7-8, is not just an emotion but an action and a choice?

_____

_____

_____

_____

_____

_____

_____

_____

_____

_____

_____

_____

_____

7. In what ways does the story challenge the characters' and readers' preconceptions about what it means to "not love" and therefore "not know God"?

_____

_____

_____

_____

_____

_____

_____

_____

_____

_____

_____

_____

_____

_____

8. How does the couple's shared faith serve as a foundation for overcoming the various challenges they face throughout their relationship?

_____

_____

_____

_____

_____

_____

_____

_____

_____

_____

_____

_____

_____

9. In what ways does the story explore the theme of personal growth through love, and how does this growth align with Christian teachings?

_____

_____

_____

_____

_____

_____

_____

_____

_____

_____

_____

_____

_____

_____

10. How does the resolution of conflicts between Chloe, Cyrus, and his family reflect the Christian principles of forgiveness and reconciliation?

_____

_____

_____

_____

_____

_____

_____

_____

_____

_____

_____

_____

"My beloved friends, let us continue to love each other since love comes from God. Everyone who loves is born of God and experiences a relationship with God. The person who refuses to love doesn't know the first thing about God, because God is love— so you can't know him if you don't love."

1 John 4:7-8
The Message Bible Translation

Stay tuned for the sensational

continuation of this Christian love story,

Divine Detours – Part 2:
The Thornton Family Saga.

Like and follow

Pearly Gates Publishing

on Facebook at

www.facebook.com/pearlygatespublishing

and the Web at www.pearlygatespublishing.com!